Andrew
Jessup

by Nette Hilton
illustrated by Cathy Wilcox

TICKNOR & FIELDS

Books for Young Readers

New York · 1993

Text copyright © 1992 by Nette Hilton   Illustrations copyright © 1992 by Cathy Wilcox   First American edition 1993 published by Ticknor & Fields,
A Houghton Mifflin company, 215 Park Avenue South, New York, New York 10003.   First published in Australia by Walter McVitty Books
For information about permission to reproduce selections from this book, write to Permissions, Ticknor & Fields,
215 Park Avenue South, New York, New York 10003.   Manufactured in the United States of America.   The text of this book is set in 15 pt. ITC Cheltenham Book.
The illustrations are watercolors reproduced in full color.   HOR 10 9 8 7 6 5 4 3 2 1

Library of Congress Cataloging-in-Publication Data   Hilton, Nette.   Andrew Jessup / by Nette Hilton ; illustrated by Cathy Wilcox.—
1st. American ed.   p.   cm.   Summary: Andrew's best friend is very disappointed when Andrew moves away, but the situation changes
when a girl moves into Andrew's old house.   ISBN 0-395-66900-6   [1. Friendship—Fiction. 2. Moving, Household—Fiction.]
I. Wilcox, Cathy, ill. II. Title.   PZ7.H56775An 1993   [E]—dc20 92-39799   CIP   AC

Andrew Jessup lived next door.
He was my very best friend.
He was my very best friend until last year.
He was my very best friend until last year because
that was when Andrew Jessup moved away.

Now Andrew Jessup lives in another place.
He goes to another school.
And he has another friend.
I know because Andrew Jessup wrote me
a letter and told me all about it.

I wish Andrew Jessup was still my friend.
Andrew Jessup used to like my stamps.
He liked to sit on my porch and
share my stamps every day.
"These are the best stamps I've ever seen,"
he used to say.

We used to bathe Fidgit together.
Andrew soaped her head.
I soaped her bottom.
I never minded, because Andrew Jessup
was my very best friend.
Fidgit didn't mind, either.

Once Andrew Jessup went with me to the zoo.
We fed the chimpanzees.
We laughed at the ostrich.
It whooshed dust all over us.
But we didn't mind, because we were
very best friends.

But now Andrew Jessup is gone.
His house is empty.
His garden is quiet.
And there's no one to look at my stamps, or
help me bathe Fidgit, or go to the zoo with me.

Sometimes I take my stamps out.

I stack them this way.

I sort them that way.

But it's not the same.

Fidgit is dirty, too.

It's very hard to wash a dog's head
and a dog's bottom when there's
just one of you. Two is better.

I wish Andrew Jessup would come back.

There are weeds growing
in Andrew Jessup's garden.
The windows don't shine anymore.
Nobody comes to visit
—except Toby the basset hound.
Sometimes he comes to sniff
under the swing.

But he doesn't stay long.
Even the smells have gone away.

Nobody comes to visit, except the man in the
gray suit. He drives up in a big, flashy car.
"Come and look at this house," he says.
And some people do.

They look at the weeds, and the dusty windows, and the empty swing. They go inside and I can hear them clomping through the rooms.
Somebody might buy the house.
But it won't be the same.
Nobody is the same as Andrew Jessup.

Some of the people have dogs.
Fidgit barks at them.
She doesn't want another dog next door.

One lady had a baby.
"Wah! Wah! Wah!" cried the baby.
"Here," I said, "look at my stamps, baby."
"WAAAAAAAAAAH!" said the baby.
I don't think I want a baby next door.

And then nobody came.
The weeds got longer.
The windows got dustier.
And the rope on the swing broke.
Nobody came.

Not until yesterday.
Yesterday, a very big truck with a
drop-down side arrived.
Yesterday, a very little car with a
very loud roar arrived.

Yesterday, Madeleine Havenblower moved in.

Madeleine Havenblower doesn't like my stamps.
"I like football," she said.
"Come and watch me kick!"

She's the best kicker
I've ever seen.
Fidgit thinks so, too.
She chased Madeleine's ball all over the yard.

She chased it through the hedge.

She chased it under the house.

And she chased it through the biggest, sloppiest

puddle in the whole backyard.

"Yuck!" said Madeleine Havenblower.
"That dog needs a bath."

Madeleine Havenblower helped me bathe Fidgit.
She soaped her bottom.
And I soaped her head.
I really liked it.
Fidgit did, too.

Tomorrow, Madeleine Havenblower
is going to the zoo with me.
We're going to feed the seals.

We're going to ride the skyway.
I think we're going to have fun.

And tomorrow night, I'm going to write
to Andrew Jessup.
I'll tell him all about my new stamp.
I'll tell him all about feeding the seals
at the zoo.
I'll tell him all about the ride
on the skyway.

And I'll tell him about his house
and the new garden
and Madeleine Havenblower because…
Madeleine Havenblower is my new
friend, but…

page 2

This is a picture of my
new stamp.
Do you like {it?

Today Madalin
Havenblower
and me wen
The man
to the zoo. say'd we cud fee
the zoo. We gave fish
seal. and

Andrew Jessup is still my very best *faraway* friend.